DARK SHANGHAI

BY

ROBERT E. HOWARD

British Library Cataloguing-in-Publication Data
A catalogue record for this book is available from the
British Library

Robert E. Howard

Robert Ervin Howard was born in Peaster, Texas in 1906. During his youth, his family moved between a variety of Texan boomtowns, and Howard – a bookish and somewhat introverted child – was steeped in the violent myths and legends of the Old South. Although he loved reading and learning, Howard developed a distinctly Texan, hardboiled outlook on the world. He became a passionate fan of boxing, taking it up at an amateur level, and from the age of nine began to write adventure tales of semi-historical bloodshed. In 1919, when Howard was thirteen, his family moved to the Central Texas hamlet of Cross Plains, where he would stay for the rest of his life.

At fifteen Howard began to read the pulp magazines of the day, and to write more seriously. The December 1922 issue of his high school newspaper featured two of his stories, 'Golden Hope Christmas' and 'West is West'. In 1924 he sold his first piece – a short caveman tale titled 'Spear and Fang' – for $16 to the not-yet-famous *Weird Tales* magazine. He published with the magazine regularly over the next few years. 1929 was a breakout year for Howard, in that the 23-year-old writer began to sell to other magazines, such as *Ghost Stories* and *Argosy*, both of whom had previously sent him hundreds of rejection slips. In 1930, he began a correspondence with weird fiction master H. P. Lovecraft which ran up to his death six years later, and is regarded as one of the great correspondence cycles in all of fantasy literature.

It was partly due to Lovecraft's encouragement that Howard created his most famous character, Conan the Cimmerian. Conan – a barbarian-turned-King during the Hyborian Age, a mythical period of some 12,000 years ago – featured in seventeen *Weird Tales* stories between 1933 and 1936, and is now regarded as having spawned the 'sword and sorcery' genre, making Howard's influence on fantasy literature comparable to that of J. R. R. Tolkien's. The Conan stories have since been adapted many times, most famously in the series of films starring Arnold Schwarzenegger.

Howard was enjoying an all-time high in sales by the beginning of 1936, but he was also deeply upset by the ill health of his mother, who had fallen into a coma. On the morning of June 11, 1936, he asked an attending nurse whether she would ever recover, and the nurse replied negatively. Howard walked to his car, parked outside the family home in Cross Plains, and shot himself. He died eight hours later, aged just thirty.

THE FIRST MAN I MET, when I stepped offa my ship onto the wharfs of Shanghai, was Bill McGlory of the Dutchman, and I should of took this as a bad omen because that gorilla can get a man into more jams than a Chinese puzzle. He says: "Well, Steve, what do we do for entertainment--beat up some cops or start a free-for-all in a saloon?"

I says: "Them amusements is low. The first thing I am goin' to do is to go and sock Ace Barlow on the nose. When I was in port six months ago somebody drugged my grog and lifted my wad, and I since found out it was him."

"Good," said Bill. "I don't like Ace neither and I'll go along and see it's well done."

So we went down to the Three Dragons Saloon and Ace come out from behind the bar grinning like a crocodile, and stuck out his hand and says: "Well, well, if it ain't Steve Costigan and Bill McGlory! Glad to see you, Costigan."

"And I'm glad to see you, you double-crossin' polecat," I says, and socked him on the nose with a peach of a right. He crashed into the bar so hard he shook the walls and a demijohn fell off a shelf onto his head and knocked him stiff, and I thought Bill McGlory would bust laughing.

Big Bess, Ace's girl, give a howl like a steamboat whistle.

"You vilyun!" she squalled. "You've killed Ace. Get out of here, you murderin' son of a skunk!" I don't know what kind of knife it was she flashed, but me and Bill left anyway. We wandered around on the waterfront most of the day and just about forgot about Ace, when all of a sudden he hove in view again, most unexpectedly. We was bucking a roulette wheel in Yin Song's Temple of Chance, and naturally was losing everything we had, including our shirts, when somebody tapped me on the shoulder. I turned around and it was Ace. I drawed back my right mauler but he said: "Nix, you numb-skull--I wanta talk business with you."

His nose was skinned and both his eyes was black, which made him look very funny, and I said: "I bet you went and blowed your nose--you shouldn't never do that after bein' socked."

"I ain't here to discuss my appearance," he said annoyedly. "Come on out where we can talk without bein' overheard."

"Foller you out into the alley?" I asked. "How many thugs you got out there with blackjacks?"

At this moment Bill lost his last dime and turned around and seen Ace and he said: "Wasn't one bust on the snoot enough?"

"Listen, you mugs," said Ace, waving his arms around like he does when excited, "here I got a scheme for makin' us all a lot of dough and you boneheads stand around makin' smart cracks."

"You're goin' to fix it so we make dough, hey?" I snorted. "I may be dumb, Ace Barlow, but I ain't that dumb. You ain't no pal of our'n."

"No, I ain't!" he howled. "I despises you! I wisht you was both in Davy Jones's locker! But I never lets sentiment interfere with business, and you two saps are the only men in Shanghai which has got guts enough for the job I got in mind."

I LOOKED AT BILL AND Bill looked at me, and Bill says: "Ace, I trusts you like I trusts a rattlesnake--but lead on. Them was the honestest words I ever heard you utter."

Ace motioned us to foller him, and he led us out of the Temple of Chance into the back of his grog-shop, which wasn't very far away. When we had set down and he had poured us some licker, taking some hisself, to show us it was on the level, he said: "Did you mutts ever hear of a man by the name of John Bain?"

"Naw," I said, but Bill scowled: "Seems like I have--naw--I can't place the name--"

"Well," said Ace, "he's a eccentric milyunaire, and he's here in Shanghai. He's got a kid sister, Catherine, which he's very fond of--"

"I see the point," I snapped, getting up and sticking the bottle of licker in my hip pocket. "That's out, we don't kidnap no dame for you. C'mon, Bill."

"That's a dirty insult!" hollered Ace. "You insinyouatin' I'd stoop so low as to kidnap a white woman?"

"It wouldn't be stoopin' for you," sneered Bill. "It would be a step upwards."

"Set down, Costigan," said Ace, "and put back that bottle, les'n you got money to pay for it.... Boys, you got me all wrong. The gal's already been kidnapped, and Bain's just about nuts."

"Why don't he go to the police?" I says.

"He has," said Ace, "but when could the police find a gal the Chineeses has stole? They'd did their best but they ain't found nothin'. Now listen--this is where you fellers come in. I know where the gal is!"

"Yeah?" we said, interested, but only half believing him.

"I guess likely I'm the only white man in Shanghai what does," he said. "Now I ask you--are you thugs ready to take a chance?"

"On what?" we said.

"On the three-thousand-dollar reward John Bain is offerin' for the return of his sister," said Ace. "Now listen--I know a certain big Chinee had her kidnapped outa her 'rickshaw out at the edge of the city one evenin'. He's been keepin' her prisoner in his house, waitin' a chance to send her up-country to some bandit friends of his'n; then they'll be in position to twist a big ransome outa John Bain, see? But he ain't had a chance to slip her through yet. She's still in his house. But if I was to tell the police, they'd raid the place and get the reward theirselves. So all you boys got to do is go get her and we split the reward three ways."

"Yeah," said Bill bitterly, "and git our throats cut while doin' it. What you goin' to do?"

"I give you the information where she is," he said. "Ain't that somethin'? And I'll do more--I'll manage to lure the big Chinee away from his house while you go after the gal. I'll fake a invitation from a big merchant to meet him somewheres--I know how to work it. An hour before midnight I'll have him away from that house. Then it'll be pie for you."

ME AND BILL MEDITATED.

"After all," wheedled Ace, "she's a white gal in the grip of the yeller devils."

"That settles it," I decided. "We ain't goin' to leave no white woman at the mercy of no Chinks."

"Good," said Ace. "The gal's at Yut Lao's house--you know where that is? I'll contrive to git him outa the house. All you gotta do is walk in and grab the gal. I dunno just where in the house she'll be, of course; you'll have to find that out for yourselves. When you git her, bring her to the old deserted warehouse on the Yen Tao wharf. I'll be there with John Bain. And listen--the pore gal has likely been mistreated so she don't trust nobody. She may not wanta come with you, thinkin' you've come to take her up-country to them hill-bandits. So don't stop to argy--just bring her along anyhow."

"All right," we says and Ace says, "Well, weigh anchor then, that's all."

"That ain't all, neither," said Bill. "If I start on this here expedition I gotta have a bracer. Gimme that bottle."

"Licker costs money," complained Ace as Bill filled his pocket flask.

"Settin' a busted nose costs money, too," snapped Bill, "so shut up before I adds to your expenses. We're in this together for the money, and I want you to know I don't like you any better'n I ever did."

Ace gnashed his teeth slightly at this, and me and Bill set out for Yut Lao's house. About half a hour to midnight we got there. It was a big house, set amongst a regular rat-den of narrow twisty alleys and native hovels. But they was a high wall around it, kinda setting it off from the rest.

"Now we got to use strategy," I said, and Bill says, "Heck, there you go makin' a tough job outa this. All we gotta do is walk up to the door and when the Chinks open it, we knock 'em stiff and grab the skirt and go."

"Simple!" I said sourcastically. "Do you realize this is the very heart of the native quarters, and these yeller-bellies would as soon stick a knife in a white man as look at him?"

"Well," he said, "if you're so smart, you figger it out."

"Come on," I said, "we'll sneak over the wall first. I seen a Chinee cop snoopin' around back there a ways and he give us a very suspicious look. I bet he thinks you're a burglar or somethin'."

Bill shoved out his jaw. "Does he come stickin' his nose into our business, I bends it into a true-lover's knot."

"This takes strategy," I says annoyedly. "If he comes up and sees us goin' over the wall, I'll tell him we're boardin' with Yut Lao and he forgot and locked us out, and we lost our key."

"That don't sound right, somehow," Bill criticized, but he's always jealous, because he ain't smart like me, so I paid no heed to him, but told him to foller me.

WELL, WE WENT DOWN a narrow back-alley which run right along by the wall, and just as we started climbing over, up bobbed the very Chinese cop I'd mentioned. He musta been follerin' us.

"Stop!" he said, poking at me with his night-stick. "What fella monkey-business catchee along you?"

And dawgoned if I didn't clean forget what I was going to tell him!

"Well," said Bill impatiently, "speak up, Steve, before he runs us in."

"Gimme time," I said snappishly, "don't rush me--lemme see now--Yut Lao boards with us and he lost his key--no, that don't sound right--"

"Aw, nuts!" snorted Bill and before I could stop him he hit the Chinee cop on the jaw and knocked him stiff.

"Now you done it!" said I. "This will get us six months in the jug."

"Aw, shut up and git over that wall," growled Bill. "We'll git the gal and be gone before he comes to. Then with that reward dough, I'd like to see him catch us. It's too dark here for him to have seen us good."

So we climbed into the garden, which was dark and full of them funny-looking shrubs the Chineeses grows and trims into all kinds of shapes like ships and dragons and ducks and stuff. Yut Lao's house looked even bigger from inside the wall and they was only a few lights in it. Well, we went stealthily through the garden and come to a arched door which led into the house. It was locked but we jimmied it pretty easy with some tools Ace had give us--he had a regular burglar's kit, the crook. We didn't hear a sound; the house seemed to be deserted.

We groped around and Bill hissed, "Steve, here's a stair. Let's go up."

"Well," I said, "I don't hardly believe we'll find her upstairs or nothin'. They proberly got her in a underground dunjun or somethin'."

"Well," said Bill, "this here stair don't go no ways but up and we can't stand here all night."

So we groped up in the dark and come into a faintly lighted corridor. This twisted around and didn't seem like to me went nowheres, but finally come onto a flight of stairs going down. By this time we was clean bewildered--the way them heathens builds their houses would run a white man nuts. So we went down the stair and found ourselves in another twisting corridor on the ground floor. Up to that time we'd met nobody. Ace had evidently did his job well, and drawed most everybody outa the house.

All but one big coolie with a meat cleaver.

WE WAS JUST CONGRATULATING ourselves when swish! crack! A shadow falling acrost me as we snuck past a dark nook was all that saved my scalp. I ducked just as something hummed past my head and sunk three inches deep into the wall. It was a meat cleaver in the hand of a big Chinee, and before he could wrench it loose, I tackled him around the legs like a fullback bucking the line and we went to the floor together so hard it knocked the breath outa him. He started flopping and kicking, but I would of had him right if it hadn't of been for Bill's carelessness. Bill grabbed a lacquered chair and swung for the Chinee's head, but we was revolving on the floor so fast his aim wasn't good. Wham! I seen a million stars. I rolled offa my victim and lay, kicking feebly, and Bill used what was left of the chair to knock the Chinaman cold.

"You dumb bonehead," I groaned, holding my abused head on which was a bump as big as a goose-egg. "You nearly knocked my brains out."

"You flatters yourself, Steve," snickered Bill. "I was swingin' at the Chinee--and there he lays. I always gits my man."

"Yeah, after maimin' all the innocent bystanders within reach," I snarled. "Gimme a shot outa that flask."

We both had a nip and then tied and gagged the Chinee with strips tore from his shirt, and then we continued our explorations. We hadn't made as much noise as it might seem; if they was any people in the house they was all sound asleep. We wandered around for a while amongst them dark or dim lighted corridors, till we seen a light shining under a crack of a door, and peeking through the keyhole, we seen what we was looking for.

On a divan was reclining a mighty nice-looking white girl, reading a book. I was plumb surprised; I'd expected to find her chained up in a dunjun with rats running around. The room she was in was fixed up very nice indeed, and she didn't look like her captivity was weighing very heavy on her; and though I looked close, I seen no sign of no chain whatever. The door wasn't even locked.

I opened the door and we stepped in quick. She jumped up and stared at us.

"Who are you?" she exclaimed. "What are you doing here?"

"Shhhhh!" I said warningly. "We has come to rescue you from the heathen!"

To my shocked surprise, she opened her mouth and yelled, "Yut Lao!" at the top of her voice.

I GRABBED HER AND CLAPPED my hand over her mouth, whilst goose-flesh riz up and down my spine.

"Belay there!" I said in much annoyance. "You wanta get all our throats cut? We're your friends, don't you understand?"

Her reply was to bite me so viciously that her teeth met in my thumb. I yelped involuntarily and let her go, and Bill caught hold of her and said soothingly, "Wait, Miss--they's no need to be scared--ow!" She hauled off and smacked him in the eye with a right that nearly floored him, and made a dart for the door. I pounced on her and she yanked out my hair in reckless handfuls.

"Grab her feet, Bill," I growled. "I come here to rescue this dame and I'm goin' to do it if we have to tie her hand and foot."

Well, Bill come to my aid and in the end we had to do just that--tie her up, I mean. It was about like tying a buzz-saw. We tore strips offa the bed-sheets and bound her wrists and ankles, as gentle as we could, and gagged her likewise, because when she wasn't chawing large chunks out of us, she would screech like a steamboat whistle. If they'd been anybody at large in the house they'd of sure heard. Honest to gosh, I never seen anybody so hard to rescue in my life. But we finally got it done and laid her on the divan.

"Why Yut Lao or anybody else wants this wildcat is more'n I can see," I growled, setting down and wiping the sweat off and trying to get my wind back. "This here's gratitude--here we risks our lives to save this girl from the clutches of the Yeller Peril and she goes and bites and kicks like we was kidnappin' her ourselves."

"Aw, wimmen is all crazy," snarled Bill, rubbing his shins where she had planted her French heels. "Dawgone it, Steve, the cork is come outa my flask in the fray and alt my licker is spillin' out."

"Stick the cork back in," I urged. And he said, "You blame fool, what you think I'd do? But I can't find the cork."

"Make a stopper outa some paper," I advised, and he looked around and seen a shelf of books. So he took down a book at random, tore out the fly-leaf and wadded it up and stuck it in the flask and put the book back. At this moment

14

I noticed that I'd carelessly laid the girl down on her face and she was kicking and squirming, so I picked her up and said, "You go ahead and see if the way's clear; only you gotta help me pack her up and down them stairs."

"No need of that," he said. "This room's on the ground floor, see? Well, I bet this here other door opens into the garden." He unbolted it and sure enough it did.

"I bet that cop's layin' for us," I grunted.

"I bet he ain't," said Bill, and for once he was right. I reckon the Chinee thought the neighborhood was too tough for him. We never seen him again.

WE TOOK THE OPPOSITE side from where we come in at, and maybe you think we had a nice time getting that squirming frail over the wall. But we finally done it and started for the old deserted warehouse with her. Once I started to untie her and explain we was her friends, but the instant I started taking off the gag, she sunk her teeth into my neck. So I got mad and disgusted and gagged her again.

I thought we wouldn't never get to the warehouse. Tied as she was, she managed to wriggle and squirm and bounce till I had as soon try to carry a boa-constrictor, and I wisht she was a man so I could sock her on the jaw. We kept to back alleys and it ain't no uncommon sight to see men carrying a bound and gagged girl through them twisty dens at night, in that part of the native quarters, so if anybody seen us, they didn't give no hint. Probably thought we was a couple of strong-arm gorillas stealing a girl for some big mandarin or something.

Well, we finally come to the warehouse, looming all silent and deserted on the rotting old wharf. We come up into the shadder of it and somebody went, "Shhhh!"

"Is that you, Ace?" I said, straining my eyes--because they wasn't any lamps or lights of any kind anywheres near and everything was black and eery, with the water sucking and lapping at the piles under our feet.

"Yeah," came the whisper, "right here in this doorway. Come on--this way--I got the door open."

We groped our way to the door and blundered in, and he shut the door and lit a candle. We was in a small room which must have been a kind of counting or checking room once when the warehouse was in use. Ace looked at the girl and didn't seem a bit surprised because she was tied up.

"That's her, all right," he says. "Good work. Well, boys, your part's did. You better scram. I'll meet you tomorrer and split the reward."

"We'll split it tonight," I growled. "I been kicked in the shins and scratched and bit till I got tooth-marks all over me, and if you think I'm goin' to leave here without my share of the dough, you're nuts."

"You bet," said Bill. "We delivers her to John Bain, personal."

ACE LOOKED INCLINED to argy the matter, but changed his mind and said, "All right, he's in here--bring her in."

So I carried her through the door Ace opened, and we come into a big inner room, well lighted with candles and fixed up with tables and benches and things. It was Ace's secret hangout. There was Big Bess and a tall, lean feller with a pale poker-face and hard eyes. And I felt the girl stiffen in my arms and kind of turn cold.

"Well, Bain," says Ace jovially, "here she is!"

"Good enough," he said in a voice like a steel rasp. "You men can go now."

"We can like hell," I snapped. "Not till you pay us."

"How much did you promise them?" said Bain to Ace.

"A grand apiece," muttered Ace, glancing at us kind of uneasy, "but I'll tend to that."

"All right," snapped Bain, "don't bother me with the details. Take off her gag."

I done so, and untied her, watching her nervously so I could duck if she started swinging on me. But it looked like the sight of her brother wrought a change in her. She was white and trembling.

"Well, my dear," said John Bain, "we meet again."

"Oh, don't stall!" she flamed out. "What are you going to do to me?"

17

Me and Bill gawped at her and at each other, but nobody paid no attention to us.

"You know why I had you brought here," said Bain in a tone far from brotherly. "I want what you stole from me."

"And you stole it from old Yuen Kiang," she snapped. "He's dead--it belongs to me as much as it does to you!"

"You've hidden from me for a long time," he said, getting whiter than ever, "but it's the end of the trail Catherine, and you might as well come through. Where's that formula?"

"Where you'll never see it!" she said, very defiant.

"No?" he sneered. "Well, there are ways of making people talk--"

"Give her to me," urged Big Bess with a nasty glint in her eyes.

"I'll tell you nothing!" the girl raged, white to the lips. "You'll pay for persecuting an honest woman this way--"

John Bain laughed like a jackal barking. "Fine talk from you, you snake-in-the-grass! Honest? Why, the police of half a dozen countries are looking for you right now!"

John Bain jumped up and grabbed her by the wrist, but I throwed him away from her with such force he knocked over a table and fell across it.

"Hold everything!" I roared. "What kind of a game is this?"

JOHN BAIN PULLED HISSELF up and his eyes was dangerous as a snake's.

"Get out of here and get quick!" he snarled. "Ace can settle with you for this job out of the ten thousand I'm paying him. Now get out, before you get hurt!"

"Ten thousand!" howled Bill. "Ace is gettin' ten thousand? And us only a measly grand apiece?"

"Belay everything!" I roared. "This is too blame complicated for me. Ace sends us to rescue Bain's sister from the Chinks, us to split a three-thousand-dollar reward--now it comes out that Ace gets ten thousand--and Bain talks about his sister robbin' him--"

"Oh, go to the devil!" snapped Bain. "Barlow, when I told you to get a couple of gorillas for this job, I didn't tell you to get lunatics."

"Don't you call us looneyticks," roared Bill wrathfully. "We're as good as you be. We're better'n you, by golly! I remember you now--you ain't no more a milyunaire than I am! You're a adventurer--that's what old Cap'n Hurley called you--you're a gambler and a smuggler and a crook in general. And I don't believe this gal is your sister, neither."

"Sister to that swine?" the girl yelped like a wasp had stung her. "He's persecuting me, trying to get a valuable formula which is mine by rights, in case you don't know it--"

"That's a lie!" snarled Bain. "You stole it from me--Yuen Kiang gave it to me before he got blown up in that experiment in his laboratory--"

19

"Hold on," I ordered, slightly dizzy, "lemme get this straight--"

"Aw, it's too mixed up," growled Bill. "Let's take the gal back where we got her, and bust Ace on the snoot."

"Shut up, Bill," I commanded. "Leave this to me--this here's a matter which requires brains. I gotta get this straight. This girl ain't Bain's brother--I mean, he ain't her sister. Well, they ain't no kin. She's got a formula--whatever that is--and he wants it. Say, was you hidin' at Yut Lao's, instead of him havin' you kidnapped?"

"Wonderful," she sneered. "Right, Sherlock!"

"Well," I said, "we been gypped into doin' a kidnappin' when we thought we was rescuin' her; that's why she fit so hard. But why did Ace pick us?"

"I'll tell you, you flat-headed gorilla!" howled Big Bess. "It was to get even with you for that poke on the nose. And what you goin' to do about it, hey?"

"I'll tell you what we're goin' to do!" I roared. "We don't want your dirty dough! You're all a gang of thieves! This girl may be a crook, too, but we're goin' to take her back to Yut Lao's! An' right off."

Catherine caught her breath and whirled on us.

"Do you mean that?" she cried.

"You bet," I said angrily. "We may look like gorillas but we're gents. They gypped us, but they ain't goin' to harm you none, kid."

20

"But it's my formula," snarled John Bain. "She stole it from me."

"I don't care what she stole!" I roared. "She's better'n you, if she stole the harbor buoys! Get away from that door! We're leavin'!"

THE REST WAS KIND OF like a explosion--happened so quick you didn't have much time to think. Bain snatched up a shotgun from somewhere but before he could bring it down I kicked it outa his hands and closed with him. I heard Bill's yelp of joy as he lit into Ace, and Catherine and Big Bess went together like a couple of wildcats.

Bain was all wire and spring-steel. He butted me in the face and started the claret in streams from my nose, he gouged at my eye and he drove his knee into my belly all before I could get started. But I finally lifted him bodily and slammed him head-first onto the floor, though, and that finished Mr. John Bain for the evening. He kind of spread out and didn't even twitch.

Well, I looked around and seen Bill jumping up and down on Ace with both feet, and I seen Catherine was winning her scrap, too. Big Bess had the advantage of weight but she was yeller. Catherine sailed into her, fist and tooth and nail, and inside of a minute Big Bess was howling for mercy.

"What I want to know," gritted Catherine, sinking both hands into her hair and setting back, "is why you and that mutt Barlow are helping Bain!"

"Ow, leggo!" squalled Big Bess. "Ace heard that Bain was lookin' for you, and Ace had found out you was hidin' at Yut Lao's. Bain promised us ten grand to get you into his hands--Bain stood to make a fortune outa the formula--and we figgered on gyppin' Costigan and McGlory into doin' the dirty work and then we was goin' to skip on the early mornin' boat and leave 'em holdin' the bag!"

"So!" gasped Catherine, getting up and shaking back her disheveled locks, "I guess that settles that!"

I looked at Bain and Ace and Big Bess, all kind of strewn around on the floor, and I said I reckon it did.

"You men have been very kind to me," she said. "I understand it all now."

"Yeah," I said, "they told us Yut Lao had you kidnapped."

"The skunks!" she said. "Will you do me just one more favor and keep these thugs here until I get a good start? If I can catch that boat that sails just at dawn, I'll be safe."

"You bet," I said, "but you can't go through them back-alleys alone. I'll go back with you to Yut Lao's and Bill can stay here and guard these saps."

"Good," she said. "Let me peek outside and see that no one's spying."

So she slipped outside and Bill picked up the shotgun and said, "Hot dawg, will I guard these babies! I hope Ace will try to jump me so I can blow his fool head off!"

"Hey!" I hollered, "be careful with that gun, you sap!"

"Shucks," he says, very scornful, "I cut my teeth on a gun--"

Bang! Again I ducked complete extinction by such a brief hair's breadth that that charge of buckshot combed my hair.

"You outrageous idjit!" I says, considerably shooken. "I believe you're tryin' to murder me. That's twice tonight you've nearly kilt me."

"Aw don't be onreasonable, Steve," he urged. "I didn't know it had a hair-trigger--I was just tryin' the lock, like this, see--"

I took the death-trap away from him and throwed it into the corner.

"Gimme a nip outa the flask," I said. "I'll be a rooin before this night's over."

I took a nip which just about emptied the flask, and Bill got to looking at the wadded-up fly-leaf which was serving as a stopper.

"Lookit, Mike," he said, "this leaf has got funny marks on it, ain't it?"

I glanced at it, still nervous from my narrer escape; it had a lot of figgers and letters and words which didn't mean nothing to me.

"That's Chinese writin'," I said peevishly. "Put up that licker; here comes Miss Deal."

She run in kind of breathless. "What was that shot?" she gasped.

"Ace tried to escape and I fired to warn him," says Bill barefacedly.

I told Bill I'd be back in a hour or so and me and the girl went out into those nasty alleys. I said, "It ain't none of my business, but would you mind tellin' me what this formula-thing is?"

"It's a new way to make perfume," she said.

"Perfume?" I snift. "Is that all?"

"Do you realize millions of dollars are spent each year on perfume?" she said. "Some of it costs hundreds of dollars an ounce. The most expensive kind is made from ambergris. Well, old Yuen Kiang, a Chinese chemist, discovered a process by which a certain chemical could be substituted for ambergris, producing the same result at a fraction of the cost. The perfume company that gets this formula will save millions. So they'll bid high.

"Outside of old Yuen Kiang, the only people who knew of its existence were John Bain, myself, and old Tung Chin, the apothecary who has that little shop down by the docks.

Old Yuen Kiang got blown up in some kind of an experiment, he didn't have any people, and Bain stole the formula. Then I lifted it off of Bain, and have been hiding ever since, afraid to venture out and try to sell it. I've been paying Yut Lao plenty to let me stay in his house, and keep his mouth shut. But now it's all rosy! I don't know how much I can twist out of the perfume companies for the formula, but I know it'll run up into the hundred thousands!"

We'd reached Yut Lao's house and I went in through a side-gate--she had a key--and went into her room the same I way me and Bill had brung her out.

"I'm going to pack and make that boat," she said. "I haven't much time. Steve--I trust you--I'm going to show you the formula. Yut Lao knows nothing about it--I wouldn't have trusted him if he'd known why I was hiding--he thinks I've murdered somebody.

"The simplest place to hide anything is the best place. I destroyed the original formula after copying it on the flyleaf of a book, and put the book on this shelf, in plain sight. No one would ever think to look there--they'd tear up the floor and the walls first--"

And blamed if she didn't pull down the very book Bill got to make his stopper! She opened it and let out a howl like a lost soul.

"It's gone!" she screeched. "The leaf's been torn out! I'm robbed!"

At this moment a portly Chinee appeared at the door, some flustered.

"What catchee?" he squalled. "Too much monkey-business!"

"You yellow-bellied thief!" she screamed. "You stole my formula!"

And she went for him like a cat after a sparrow. She made a flying leap and landed right in his stummick with both hands locked in his pig-tail. He squalled like a fire-engine as he hit the floor, and she began grabbing his hair by the handfuls.

A BIG CLAMOR RIZ in some other part of the house. Evidently all Yut Lao's servants had returned too. They was jabbering like a zoo-full of monkeys and the clash of their knives turned me cold.

I grabbed Catherine by the slack of her dress and lifted her bodily offa the howling Yut Lao which was a ruin by this time. And a whole passel of coolies come swarming in with knives flashing like the sun on the sea-spray. Catherine showed some inclination of going to the mat with the entire gang--I never see such a scrapping dame in my life--but I grabbed her up and racing across the room, plunged through the outer door and slammed it in their faces.

"Beat it for the wall while I hold the door!" I yelled, and Catherine after one earful of the racket inside, done so with no more argument. She raced acrost the garden and begun to climb the wall. I braced myself to hold the door and crash! a hatchet blade ripped through the wood a inch from my nose.

"Hustle!" I yelled in a panic and she dropped on the other side of the wall. I let go and jumped back; the door crashed outwards and a swarm of Chineeses fell over it and piled up in a heap of squirming yeller figgers and gleaming knives. The sight of them knives lent wings to my feet, as the saying is, and I wish somebody had been timing me when I went acrost that garden and over that wall, because I bet I busted some world's speed records.

Catherine was waiting for me and she grabbed my hand and shook it.

"So long, sailor," she said. "I've got to make that boat now, formula or not. I've lost a fortune, but it's been lots of fun. I'll see you some day, maybe."

"Not if I see you first, you won't," I said to myself, as she scurried away into the dark, then I turned and run like all get-out for the deserted warehouse.

I was thinking of the fly-leaf Bill McGlory tore out to use for a stopper. Them wasn't Chinese letters--them was figgers--technical symbols and things! The lost formula! A hundred thousand dollars! Maybe more! And since Bain stole it from Yuen Kiang which was dead and had no heirs, and since Catherine stole it from Bain, then it was as much mine and Bill's as it was anybody's. Catherine hadn't seen Bill tear out the sheet; she was lying face down on the divan.

I gasped as I run and the sweat poured off me. A fortune! Me and Bill was going to sell that formula to some perfume company and be rich men!

I didn't keep to the back-alleys this time, but took the most direct route; it was just getting daylight. I crossed a section of the waterfront and I seen a stocky figger careening down the street, bellering, "Abel Brown the sailor." It was Bill.

"Bill McGlory." I said sternly, "you're drunk!"

"If I wasn't I'd be a wonder!" he whooped hilariously. "Steve, you old sea-horse, this here's been a great night for us!"

"Where's Ace and them?" I demanded.

"I let 'em go half an hour after you left," he said. "I got tired settin' there doin' nothin'."

"Well, listen, Bill," I said, "where abouts is that--"

"Haw! Haw! Haw!" he roared, bending over and slapping his thighs. "Lemme tell you somethin'! Steve, you'll die laughin'! You knew old Tung Chin which runs a shop down on the waterfront, and stays open all night? Well, I stopped there to fill my flask and he got to lookin' at that Chineese writin' on that paper I had stuffed in it. He got all excited and what you think? He gimme ten bucks for it!"

"Ten bucks!" I howled. "You sold that paper to Tung Chin?"

"For ten big round dollars!" he whooped. "And boy, did I licker up! Can you imagine a mutt payin' good money for somethin' like that? What you reckon that sap wanted with that fool piece of paper? Boy, when I think how crazy them Chineese is--"

And he's wondering to this day why I hauled off and knocked him stiffer than a red-brick pagoda.

THE END